I0638802

Ballet For Murderers

being the Escape, Travels and final
Downfall of a Murderer

by

Richard Wayne Horton

Acknowledgements

"Bullets & Horses," "Cat," and "The Expatriate" appeared in Meat For Tea The Valley Review.

"Cocoon" appeared in The Bitchin' Kitsch.

"How Humor Works" appeared in Southern Pacific Review.

Published by Human Error Publishing
Paul Richmond
www.humanerrorpublishing.com
paul@humanerrorpublishing.com

ISBN: 978-1-948521-08-6

Cover:
Beth Filson, black and white clayboard etching,
"What Death Is: When The Trees Want Back Their Own Heart."

Front and back cover design:
Tam Fricke

Table Of Contents

Argumentum

The Murderer begins as a Director at a
detention center. The Americans come.
What! This isn't America already? No, it's
old days in Central Europe. He's a Nazi.
Crazy!

He escapes to NY and becomes a hero to
hoodlums

But then he settles down to a mickey-
mouse career as a company exec. Funny

How evil men can end up in leadership.
Did I see you jump with surprise just
then? Anyway at long last

The Nazi hunters find him but whaddya
know! He escapes again like always, and
starts on a life of flight.

From a grimy bus seat he sees magnificent
scenery pass his window, double exposed
on a memory screen that offers testimony
in a trial that never took place.

It has to end, though. If you're like me

You know how endings work.

Is This A Comic Book?

Murderers are often charming. Aren't they
sweet?

But even if they aren't,

Even if they're fairly dreadful,

You may be charmed by them when you
pick up a comic book in which their lives
are celebrated in brightly colored cells.
Red. Black. Yellow. Thick black lines
around the chin, the mouth, the eyes.

But as you fall in love with the murderer,
you should be aware that you can expect a
wallop of terror when you go to asleep that
night,

The night of the day,

When you found the comic book, perhaps
on a forest path, or maybe in your front
yard after it was thrown from the window
of a speeding car.

Yes, when you close your eyes that night,
other eyes

Will open.

They are directly above you.

They have found you.

The Murderer Flees

At the detention center, the Lieutenant walks into the Murderer's office to show him his comic novel about zany detention center personalities. But what's this? The Americans are about to drive through the front gate. Will they obstruct the budding writer's path to publication?

Three objects on the Murderer's desk.

Object one: a harmless chocolate.

Object two: a cyanide capsule.

Object three: a revolver.

The Lieutenant nabs the chocolate. The Murderer says, "Always the easy way!" The junior officer steps out the door.

Back in the office, bang! No more Murderer.

Just then the Yanks drive through the gate. The Lieutenant waves and offers the chocolate. Ratta-tat-tat! Now hold on, fellas!

It's discovered later that the Lieutenant really was a comic wizard. Couple of movie scripts. Modern jazz ballet musical. That bastard could write!

But what if the Murderer only staged his suicide?
What if he really got away and went to New York?

The Murderer In NY

Hep, now, my beat cats!

In the alley, some leather-jacketed no-goods divide out the currency from the zippered leather pouch filched from a shopkeep. Now these are serious hoods, cat, even if they look like ballet dancers.

One hood looks up from the mathematix, eyeballs the dark alley and raises a hand for silence. Footsteps approach. Look out! It's the Murderer!

Everyone knows the Murderer. The hoodlums step aside to let their hero pass. They doff their motorcycle caps, but the Murderer fronts up, grabs the pack leader by the jacket, jerks him around, and slaps him. "Gonna kill me? Huh? Gonna kill me?"

The Cap'n's considering it, but just then the Detective steps out from the shadow of a doorway. The hoods run.

The Murderer glares at the dour gumshoe. "What do you know now?" he asks. "Do you know enough?"

The Murderer's Christmas Party

Deck the halls! It's Christmas of 1953. At the party the Shrink is telling the Murderer to forget the past, and the poor Murderer's tried, God knows, but unwanted memories are hard to shake. His wife and boss have both complained he "kills" the holiday mood.

And then there's that Detective who keeps hanging around. "Get rid of the Detective!" yell wife, mother-in-law and boss at the same time, as they bring in the snack platter and kids blow paper horns.

Someone opens the door, pulls the Detective in and gives him a drink. "Lighten up!" yells the party-goer at the dour gumshoe.

After the production awards are handed out, everyone sings holiday songs. The sweating, hollow-eyed Murderer is smiling falsely, the song leaflet in front of his face, his voice cracking on the high notes, and the grimly festive Detective is up on a tall ladder tying the star to the top of the tree. The Murderer's wife is at the foot of the ladder steadying it, smiling upward.

The Shrink comes to give the wife a hand. He shouts encouragement to her above the party noise, then he adds that in his opinion the Murderer should get rid of the Detective, the Murderer doesn't need the Detective. The ladder shakes, and the Murderer's wife grips it more firmly. The Detective looks down at his two helpers, his eyes extremely watchful.

Later at home, the sweating hollow-eyed Murderer stands in T-shirt and boxer shorts brushing his teeth at the bathroom mirror as his wife,

The Murderer's wife,

Blandly pulls down the bedspread revealing Santa Clause pillowcases. The Murderer appears in the doorway. "I'm feeling frisky!" he says, his mouth smiling horribly, his eyes shocked and remorseful.

Outside the apartment complex, beneath a tree, the Detective lights a cigarette.

The Murderer's Lifetime Achievement Award

It's thirty years later. Everyone's on stage and the the Murderer's pal, the Shrink, gets up and and goes to the mic. The Murderer scoots his chair close to his wife's. As the Shrink begins his introduction, someone notices that canned music is still playing on the overhead speakers, and runs to turn it off. On and on drones the doc, as the Murderer turns to the chair on his <u>other</u> side, where the Detective, looking no older than always,
is smiling for once in his life.

"Why, you old so-and-so!" says the Murderer. "I knew you could crack a smile!"

"Who are you talking to?" asks his wife.

The Detective speaks, something he's also never done before. "I know enough now!" he says.

The Murderer starts to smile, before it hits him. Then he glances toward the double doors in back of the semi-darkened auditorium, where a group of elderly people with horrified faces have come in, flanked by policemen. More policemen quietly enter.

Hey it's all up for that Murderer, huh?
But wait! Wha' happened? He got away!
Slippery son of a bitch, aint he?

Newspapers Stalk
The Murderer

The newspaper spreads to the horizon, an
outstretched arm of paper, black letters
that crackle in the wind.

MURDERER STILL AT LARGE

A reader turns the page, only to have
it wrap around his arm and cling like a
sentimental joke. Later, he's seen walking
through the rain wrapped in a cocoon of
wet newspaper pulp.

The rustling at the Murderer's door grows
louder. The newspapers have come.
Drawing his revolver he holds them off
long enough to blockade the door with
realist furniture. Boards across a window:
A bent nail.

Outside, another truck stops and newspapers blow from its bed toward his door.

Yikes! He's out the back window!

Kinda funny, when you think about it.

The idea that gettn' caught, servin' jail
time, goin' to the electric chair

Means shit.

The Murderer's Old Lover

I think of you   a glass of wine   2 years
old
Un(drunk!)

It happens in damp rooms. A memory
rolls down her face.

...wasting away...

A hand on her forehead trails fingers.

Can a tinkle of ice   heard over the phone
Trigger the avalanche?

Good-bye.

What was that terrible word you said?

The Murderer's Train Trip

The train freighted with pleasure
Exploding ice refreshment
Roars into the don't tell me
Hospital
Kill that
The night outside the window
Is a coke on ice
All I get from phonefriends
Is a loose shoulder platitude
There'll be more and more and more
Meantime several bullets
Make their point hammering
Into the same TV soldier.
That's prose for you.
Redundant.
That's prose for you...
I already said that.

Surfaces observed
Dissolve into the distance.
If you will not resist
You will not exist.

The Murderer Tries To Hide Out

Strange and far was his cabin. It faced
the wrong direction and stood beside the
wrong lake. The fish there were made of
air. Which reminds me. Don't look up.

The Murderer Hops A Bus

The bus driver stepped up into the bus,
saw a sailor and thought fate or poverty.

A lady was talking about what a shit she
was. Her daughter was there, agreeing. "I
really ought to be tied up and beat on! I
aint no good!"

The murderer spoke up: "That could be
arranged."

The bus station started sliding backward.
The driver's head carefully looked both
ways as the sunlight painted it faded
sunshade green. He thought, "We're
eeeeeeeeeeasing out of the station now.
Take it easy."

Brick warehouses, a sign saying "Peep
Shows!" The front of a cafe. At the counter earlier the sailor told a plump Black
woman she had a bread crumb on the corner of her mouth, and she looked at him,
grave and lovely.

He wanted to suggest he and she could...
well, you know...but then he saw the bus
pulling in across the street, oh crap!

An old man with his peter hanging out
passed the cafe window just then, on his
way to a red candy shop sign depicting
pretty teenage girls.

He sang, "It's coooold outside!   But so sweeeet inside!"

The Murderer Looks At A Cloud

In the motionless hot air beside a road
smudged with tar, trees sing subconscious-
ly. There's a big house nearby, a drink of
water from a garden hose. Beyond that, a
yellow hay field. Beneath the field, a naked
beating noise

Up in the sky the clouds are chariots of
pink ice cream. A child king rides them all
day, calling across vast distances.

I   see   you!

The Murderer Gripes About His Childhood

Thin twisty poor that's what we were.
The nose would get twisted around. The
clothes...Wrinkles wouldn't come out of
them, they were twisted, like everything
else. Like me. Surprise, surprise!

Someone somewhere had grabbed the
sky and was pulling it out of shape. The
buildings were wrinkled. The world was
sideways.

In Bed With Bombs

Lights out in the aftermath of beans, the brothers lay in bed hitting each other. Outside, war was raging. The bomber, a crying saint shed tears that shattered a church window, completing it.

The Murderer Sees A Prison

What is a prison?

The bricks stack up to make a tower, a
monument to constipation. Fear glazes
the bricks and the chaos trapped inside
roars its endless question. But from the
outside the tower only glares with its
mouth clamped shut.

A woman nearby with a scowl carries a
purse with its mouth clamped shut, and
only opens it to do dental work.

At Mama's House
Everything Was An Antique

The Murderer remembers. His mom
painted everything in her house. She
painted the shadows. She loved them so.
The kitchen wall was golden ocher.

Tired of card games with noisy cousins, the
plink of coins in a coffee can, the Murderer
came to stand by the kitchen sink, looking
out the window. Ivory clouds passed in a
golden blue sky. Could there have been
a sweet romance here once? Maybe the
piano played Schubert. But then the lovers
died! The mother wore a black rose. He
turned on the faucet and held a glass under it, allowing it to fill, and then overflow.

How long would his fingers rise through
the water?

Death Of The Murderer

The bus had been making wrong turns and
the driver wouldn't listen when the Murderer objected. The Murderer yelled, "I
could teach you a lesson!"

The driver shook his head and said, "You
can't threaten me."

"It's not a threat. It's a promise!"

"My mistake." The driver exchanged a
smile with one of the passengers.

Another wrong turn. The murderer yelled,
"I could kill you in a heartbeat! I've done
it before!"

"Oh, please! Be my guest!"

The Murderer fell silent. His silences
had once been feared. A predatory smile
positioned itself on his face. His old smile.
Back from storage.

The bus swerved madly. Wrong. Wrong.
Wrong.

Dismay replaced the hunter's smile. "Stop,
I tell you! I've grown tired of my trip!"

"As you wish. If I were you...but I'm not!
Very well, then. Not my idea of the perfect
destination, but I'm not a murderer, am

I?" The bus pulled to the curb beneath a giant elm tree. The door clattered open. "Watch your step, Sir!"

On a sidewalk at midnight, the Murder watched the bus pull away. He waved a disgusted hand at it, then turned. Before him rose an iron gate with letters worked into its grillwork.

WANDERER'S RETURN

The Murderer Meets The Terrible Child

The murderer has outwitted his pursuers.

And here's the kicker. The moment they
started to chase him
they showed they didn't understand what
the real chase was.

He sits on a gravestone as the sun rises one
more time over the cemetary. He starts
hearing a voice nearby. There's a kid out
there messing around among the stones,
talking to himself.

"My parents are being good today. They
came out earlier to watch me. I told them
the conditions were right. But they only
shrugged.

"I have special gifts!

"I can push subtly upward and float above
the grass between the stones. You stones!
See how I surmount you? Now I permit
myself to drift to earth. I don't have to,
but I choose it. I'll walk to the house and
climb the steps just as a normal child
would do."

The Murderer listens. The kid makes a
quiet ratcheting sound. The Murderer
thinks it might be laughter.

"I will impress my parents. See? I'm step-
ping off the top step and floating outward
continuing to make walking motions.
Hah! Steps are not for me!

"My parents – what are they doing?
They're walking back into the house!

"IS THAT HOUSE BETTER THAN ME?
IT IS A GRAVE, DO YOU HEAR?

"They're gone now, but still I hang in the
air. They can't stop me! Slowly I rotate
forward. Rotate. Revolve. Revolution.
The rule of revolution is that you cannot
look into the sky when it is below you,

"or it will become hungry.

"You're still here. You don't ignore me as
my parents do. Come with me. I'll show
you something. Oh, I'm so excited!

"Now we're on a hill. Look where I'm
pointing! A panorama! There are fields
over there full of wheat. Take my hand.
We step from the hilltop and now we're
flying!

"As long as you clutch some part of me,
you won't fall to your death.

"You didn't know that, did you?

"What if I were to become like a cloud and

start to dissolve?

"Yes, hold on tighter. I like that we're bet-ter friends now.

"We're passing over the wheat, very low. I brush my hand against it. See? Like that! Now I will show you an orchard. Do you like peaches and apples? We will drift among the trees. Try to pick an apple! I can!

"What have you done? You're clinging to that tree!
You've broken contact! Now you'll miss it! You look silly back there hugging a branch. Good-bye. You were a bad friend, and now you won't get to go over the cliff with me.

"Now I'm going over the cliff!

"There is a deep blue space below. If I were a normal child I would be afraid. Being afraid might be fun. But it's not for me.

"The expanding shape below is fascinating. Now I see the sparkle of the waves. Oh, look! Rocks! I'll stop just short of them and begin slowly

"To rise.

"I wonder what it would feel like if I were to swallow the earth.

"Hello there, you walking on the beach. Should I swallow it? No?

"Hm.

"I'll rise now and go home. I had a conversation! Oh, I'm so sociable!

"Here I am again at the orchard. The wanderer's return. Look who I've found! You're still here, bad friend!

"You used to be a murderer.

"If you knew all the things I've been, you would be impressed.

"I know where there's a path to lower places. Come with me. This is fun! Come on!

"I will allow no more disobedience.

"I must say, for a murderer, you're awfully frightened."

In The Lower Places

Now, reader, you will hear with surprise an account of the Murderer's progress in the lower places where his guide, the Terrible Child, impresses him with his special abilities to pass through stone or metal walls by merely leaning against them till they submit.

Also through fires do the two souls venture, unconsumed.

They come at length to a chamber where ardents, or eyes, or little flames innumerable, circle in a gallery. Or perhaps their circling itself is the gallery. Or perhaps there is no gallery. The Terrible Child remarks, "I have joined their rout at times and made to eat them, but they had no taste or meaning."

At that, the Murderer says, "I will go to them."

The Terrible Child says, "Take my hand then."

They rise and join the rout, the Terrible Child indifferent but the Murderer possessed, for the ardents are portals. They are souls. They are love. They are knowledge. They are eyes. They have found him. He has found his downfall. Eternal love for what he has killed.

Here Ends (Doesn't End)
The Ballet For Murderers

Five Stories

By

Richard W. Horton

How Humor Works

Some information about Brownson, KS in August of 1937: there's a decent hotel, a fine eating establishment, and a grassy park next to the court house where you'll see the bronze statue of Orestes Brownson, and a WWI howitzer. If you are of a certain age, exercise care when climbing on the gun. It once killed people. There are no parking meters in town, but there are hitching posts, largely ignored these days. What else can I say? The Brownson Tigers are likely to beat Lawrence this year. There's a literary salon that gathers above McGee's Book Store Wednesdays. Bet you thought you could call us hicks! Naw!

1. **At The Gym**

Penny McGee got under the bleachers in the gym with her broom, and the noises it made smacking into things must have alerted one of the speaker's prep men. He came running and peeked under at her, holding his suit jacket closed, so he wouldn't scare her with the black leather holster under his arm. He couldn't help smiling, seeing as how she was a dish.

She glared. "What?"

He said, "Just checkin'!"

She thought, checkin' what? And who was this bird that was coming, this lefty speaker? How did he rate prep guys? One thing she knew: the union rep didn't like him. She finished, got out and worked the pile down the front of the bleachers to the trash cans not too far from the microphone. Ed asked the prep guy: "Ever play any basketball?"

"No, but I follow the Chicago team."

"Is that where the funny man is from?"

"Mr. Paulsen? No, he's from New York." While saying it, he glanced at Penny again.

She said, "What are you looking at? You're like him, like Paulsen! A letcher!"

"Sorry. You were lookin', so I looked. I won't mash on you, Penny! Not unless you want me to!"

"I'll deck you if you try!"

Later as she rushed home to change (because the staff had been given free tickets), she wondered why the prep guy had known her name. Maybe he also knew she'd voted for the President in '36, even though her sister Lu-Ann belonged to the John Reed Club and would have voted for Stalin if he'd run.

2. At The Hotel

In room 1b at the Worthington Hotel in cozy downtown Brownson, Jack Paulsen had his note pad out. He was hunched

over a little table next to his bed, his long
legs, in light brown slacks, sticking out.
He was smiling. It must have been one
of the jokes he would put in his speech
about the psychology of humor. But no, I
take that back. It was a line that would go
in a letter to Leon Davidovich Trotsky in
Mexico. He knew Trotsky
would wrinkle his nose and be impatient
if he tried to joke with him in his letter.
Then Leon Davidovich's wife would worry
that he might have eaten something nasty.

Then...Jack did actually remember a joke,
and began deconstructing it on the note-
pad.

Jack had mailed copies of his 1936 humor
book to Charlie Chaplin, Groucho Marx,
Stan Laurel, Oliver Hardy, Walt Disney, H.
L. Mencken, James Thurber, a psychology
professor at U MI, and one at Columbia.
He did not mail one to Leon Davidovich
Trotsky, though he was sorely tempted,
just to get the bearded guy's goat. He
mentioned the book to Mary McCarthy,
but then felt pathetic, holding a drink and
hawking a book at a Partisan Review party
where people were trying to have fun. A
little later, Mary climbed on his lap anyway.

The old socialist magazine he used to run,
which was now Stalinist, had squirted bird
droppings on the new book, with a review

called, "What?? And Why??" The review-
er used to be a dear sweet friend. A lover
really. Back in the misty past.

3. **Meanwhile In Moscow**

Over in Moscow, Stalin was on the toilet
reading a paperback, not Paulsen's, and a
security wonk was outside the door talking
about Paulsen. Josef Vissarionovich said,
"Who?"

"The 'Lenin Testament' guy."

"I didn't read it. How is it?"

"...ah!...understood! Anyway, some nut in
Kansas wants to off Paulsen."

"He does? Interesting. I heard Paulsen
was on the move. Trying to escape his
many failures, I imagine."

"Yes."

"Now he's even been smoked out of New
York! Astonishing! The useless loafer
thinks there's a gold field in the central
and western departments of the United
States. But in the American West, there
are cowboys who shoot guns at each other.
Dangerous place!" The toilet paper roll
spun noisily. Stalin chuckled. "Instead
of gold he might find lead. Well! I always
knew he was a species of alchemist! Here!

Take this!" Stalin handed the paperback out of the partially opened door. On the cover was a pretty secretary, a train, the Eiffel Tower, and a crouching gangster holding a gun. The toilet flushed loudly.

4. **At The Hotel, Kansas, U.S.A.**

If Paulsen had guessed what Mr. Smiles had just said about him, he would of course have deconstructed it and written a note to self.

5. At The Gym, Then It Flips To Topeka, 1917

Out at the high school grounds, the mayor and assistant mayor came walking out of the gym. The fat jovial mayor turned around and looked at the huge brick barn, which is what the gym looked like, and shook his head. The little town of Brownson hadn't funded a municipal auditorium, when they learned there might be a WPA grant in the offing. But Jack Paulsen settling for a small town HS gym? That was sad. He used to get big civic centers overflowing with mad-as-hell laborers yelling and raising their fists when he told them Wilson's war would not only yank them away from their nests and stuff them into uniforms, but when they came back their wages would be too low to live on. Get you going, and get you coming! Now that's a doggone shame!

In 1917 the mayor had been a college
kid. He'd taken the bus to Topeka to hear
Paulsen, though all his relatives, the den-
tist, the doctor, school chums and mom
& dad wanted America to go on and fight,
and get it over with.

Patriot gangs were meeting near the
auditorium, singing songs, slapping each
other's backs, and handing out lead pipes
and baseball bats. They had an American
answer to Paulsen's communist yappings.
Yeah, he was a Bolshie! You couldn't be
stupid enough not to know that!

Paulsen's host family had put their gassed-
up automobile at their back door in case
Paulsen had to escape during the night.

The 19 year old future mayor got to the civic auditorium and heard Paulsen, or tried
to. The lanky, handsome speaker with his
long face and thick light brown hair had to
raise his voice to be heard, but otherwise
looked bored and a little amused. "Wear-
ers of overalls and big shoes," he said, "are,
or should be, the deciders in the new world
which is being born. Events in Russia
in October of this year, have proved that
laborers have the brains to be their own
bosses. The Russian Duma is now a work-
er's council, dispensing wise decisions.

"But what's happening right here in the
U. S. of A.?" And here he held his hand

laconically out, palm up. "Working stiffs
– not you, my friends, but everybody else
– workers, I say, are getting all hopped
up and rushing down to enlist and put on
a uniform to do the business of tycoons
who want to shake the tree, or the dice –
overseas, over there, yes, over there! And
suppose those boys get their head shot off,
why – the tycoons will just wave the flag
some more – your flag, not theirs, they
stole it – and Johnnie will come home in a
box. Now..."

Yells and whistles erupted, just as the
doors in back of the auditorium banged
open and men in checkered shirts carrying
clubs and flags marched in singing "On-
ward Christian Soldiers."

From the curtains, the organizers were
hissing and waving at Paulsen trying to get
him to stop talking and come over where
they could get him out of the building. It
was winter and one of them was holding
a coat open for him to get into. An automobile was chugging out in the snow, but
Paulsen started talking again, welcoming
the new arrivals. "There's room enough
here for us all, friends!" And on and on.
The roughnecks were a little puzzled that
he didn't try to run off. They figured they
were going to get him anyway, so they
stopped to listen, just for the hell of it.

Turned out, they had grievances too, and

he was very sympathetic, a kind of sleek
greyhound up there on the stage, who
could talk like a hickory-handled Sigmund
Freud. He'd read everything by Freud,
and grafted it to vaudeville and hard-cider
populism, and now the plugs were telling
him their troubles and he was just spin-
ning their wheel.

Later on, when he was in the little Ford,
more or less escaping, you might say,
the plugs shook their heads and woke up
plenty sore, ran out and piled on a truck
to chase him, but it was too late. Damn
dangerous business, pacifism!

6. At The Hotel

Back at the Worthington, Paulsen got up
and opened his window. He leaned on the
sill and looked out at the sunny, sleepy
town, his nose coming close to the screen,
which smelled like dust and iron. There
were shrubs, a curb, round-shaped cars.
He could see a little ways up the street.

There'd been a get-together the previous
night at the Mayor's mansion, and a pair
of eyes had come close. A mouth under
the eyes had said something in an unconcerned way, and cocked ironic. He'd been
unconcerned too. Just let it play. Women
read men fairly accurately. Her name was
Sally. She wanted him to know her name
and not call her "Hey, you!" She also

wanted him to know she knew.

About him.

"Oh, that! Those stories!" (And he chuckled).

"Mm-hmmm!"

"Well, Sally..."

And segue to the hotel room, and his long
face looking out at the street. Looking
downward. The wrist watch came floating
up. 3:20. There was a soft crunch outside
somewhere. Someone getting out of a car.
OK, then, here we go!

In 1920 Paulsen had been in Europe.
Having read everything he could find by
Freud, Adler and Jung, he'd gone to visit a
somewhat cranky Freud, who had received
one of Paulsen's books in the mail, the one
debunking marriage, freeing the sex act
from shame, and proposing obligation-
free serial sexual experiences. Paulsen
found himself dismissed and walking out
the door before he said, "Wait a minute!
There are other topics, you know!" And
he verbally fought his way back in, as the
old man waved a hand disgustedly and
said, "Very well, have it your way, but
you're not going to like what I have to
say. But first..." (and he made a gracious
bow which was almost convincing) "...
thank you for your...reconstructions of my

case studies. You shouldn't have!" And Freud handed back Paulsen's book, bound in dark red Morocco. Paulsen raised his palm. "No! No! It's inscribed to you, Herr Doctor! It's yours!"

With a sigh of regret, Freud put the book back on his desk. "Now Mr. Paulsen, you may not believe it, but I feel affection for all my patients, and I sincerely wish for them a satisfactory adjustment and return to health. I help them, with their own words, to medicate themselves. But in your case, that would be a bad idea. You would simply pull yourself apart!"

Paulsen was smiling now. A game! A game! Freud noticed, and sighed. "You have in your little book picked apart my ideas. That's fine. But where's the resolution? Sex, now. Yes, sexual urges must be acknowledged. But must there then be an abandonment of every relationship afterward? Are we not to hold together in any fashion? Are we not to own anything? I have children and a wife, Mr. Paulsen. I'm not the best of fathers or the best husband, but I am here! I am here! You are creating in your wake a psychological junk yard."

Socialism and free love. It was all about not owning anything, but it was more than that. Freud was right, but he was wrong too, as Paulsen explained later in his deconstruction of his talk with Freud.

Paulsen would be the first to admit the free love conclusions he had come to were a patchwork beast. And was it <u>free</u> free love, or was he a piece of furniture for the rebellious, the temporarily lonely, and the hedonistic?

There was a soft knock on the door.

At 4:30, after the events in the room, whatever they might have been, Sally said, "Can I have this?"

Jack, who was putting on a tie, said, "Yeah. It's fluff, though." She folded and pocketed the scrap of paper. It really was fluff. On the scrap:

> I experience (it)
> I am not placed
> I do not own what I do
> It's not even a what
> It's doing

Hey, you know, maybe the guy has a point in that last line. You think?

7. The McGee Apartment

Penny McGee and her husband (and sister and mama) lived in a walk-up next to the laundry. The apt. had a window looking down on the street, and the girls were gossipy. Penny's sister Lu-Ann was at work at the bookstore down the street. There had been a storage room upstairs from the bookstore, but it had been cleaned and swept. Lu-Ann was a poet who had friends who wrote, one of whom, Chester, was Lu-Ann's fiance. So that space up there was used for Wednesday night poetry readings, though boxes and supplies were still stored there too, kind of over in a corner. It was Chester's idea to put a hand-lettered sign in the front window: "John Reed Club."

The poetry readings, well, yeah, you could read poetry all right, and it didn't have to be political, but if the reader suddenly started bellyaching about the Moscow trials, or saying where, oh where, did pure revolution go, or calling Stalin a dirty dog, the other poets sitting around in wooden folding chairs, and Chester standing over by the literature table, would have to educate the guy or gal making all that racket.

Anyway, Penny walks into her apartment, and her mama, sitting by the window, says, "The English teacher has her car parked in front of Spruell's."

"That's nice. Did Henry telephone and say he would come to Paulsen's talk?"

The mom looked disappointed. No bite on the English teacher. "Nope. Guess he'll stay late."

"Well, darn! I'll get letched to death at that speech and then won't have anybody to eat with at Spruell's after that."

"I'll go if I have to."

"Well, you better hurry up and get a dress on. I'm going over to Lu-Ann's."

"Why?"

"I want to see if the bookstore has anything by Jack Paulsen."

8.   At McGee's Bookstore

In the bookstore Penny yelled, "Jack Paulsen!
P-A-U-L-S-E-N!"

"Don't know any writer named Jack Polecat. I could ask Lu-Ann...Lu-Ann!" Jerry, the assistant, had put his hands to his mouth and called his boss like she was on the other side of a mountain. She was right next to him, taking books out of a box.

"We don't have any polecats in this store, sister!" she said.

9. At Spruell's

The mayor's car pulled up and parked in back of Sally Donaldson's 1931 Plymouth. Sally, walking breezily toward it, stopped and found something interesting to look at in the boot shop window. She was much too pretty and female to be looking at work boots, so she backtracked a little, and checked out the bookshop window. Now here was something Jack might be interested in. <u>Lessons Of The Second International</u>. Should she assign it to her class? Maybe not.

The assistant mayor got out first, stretched, and rubbed his stomach. The mayor got out. "Yes-sir!" said the assistant mayor. "Smart idea, boss! I didn't eat breakfast or lunch either!" The mayor passed him and went into Spruell's. The assistant looked up the street, saw Sally looking at books, went "Mm-mm!" and went in. Sally waited a few moments, then moved toward her car. The mayor would be greeting the other early bird diners, and haw-hawing. She slipped into her car and drove off.

Otis, the proprietor, seated the 2 men in white shirts with rolled up sleeves at the table by the front window. The assistant mayor said, "I speck Brownson is going to whip Lawrence this year!" Two guys in the nearby booth liked the sound of that, so there was noisy basketball talk for a while, then the 2 guys got up and left, and the assistant said,. "What's the deal with Paulsen?"

"Well, his book royalties are down and he has some bills. He invested in a film about the Romanovs and the other guy hogged the profits. It's just a little setback, but he figured, what the heck, I like the heartland, I like the people there, they always say howdy and I'm not getting that in New York, noooooo! A friend told him, don't be so predictable, Jack, there are people out there now who would just love to catch you strolling across Union Square after midnight, now, you're scaring me, Jack, being so predictable!

"Old Uncle Joe over in Moscow didn't like it one bit when Jack split the whole wide world in half by saying Stalin, Kamenev, Zinoviev and the others already had a machine going while Lenin was on his death bed. Roughnecks and psychopaths were let loose even as Lenin's coffin was rolling down the avenue toward the mausoleum. Jack's book even caught Trotsky by surprise. Trotsky had still been in Moscow wearing his commander's uniform, trying to make nice with Stalin, but that went to hell.

Just as Jack was saying the Revolution was dead in Russia, Stalin latched onto his world network and I mean <u>hard</u>. The idea was, look, Stalinism is alive, it's there, you look at it and it looks back at you. What do you want? Ask Stalin. Maybe he'll get it for you. Ask the purists, ask Trotsky and he'll tell you to go to the

moon! Jack came back from Russia, and, oh, they had a banquet for him at a big hall! Five people showed up! Jack's like... wha...?

His publisher was as good as gold, taking a hit on Jack's next few books. They were communist books that communists didn't read. Jack knew it, so he saw no reason to toe any line. He said Marx wasn't Jesus. He was a scholar. An organization was a good as its people. Americans had the know-how to get out and get under the Marxist automobile and make it work in Detroit, in Denver, or in Podunk. Eventually he found himself asking the ultimate question: is it simply impossible to get workers to run a country, even if the machine doesn't move in? Maybe unions are the best anyone can do!"

Otis said, "You guys quit plotting, now!" and set their house platters down by their coffees.

"So now it's humor!" said his assistant.

"Humor in America! God, yes! That sells!"

10. At Kansas Custodial

Out on Route 30, at Kansas Custodial, the window guys were picking up their supplies and tools. Contract with Brownson I.S.D. to do the windows on the school gym, the ones high up on the wall, Aug. 15, 1937.

How to get up there? Well, a contact at the school had hung a catwalk under the whole row of windows on the west wall.

Should have been the east wall, for tactical reasons, but the east wall faced the highway, which would be getting some traffic as the custodians were trying to set up. Someone might even tell them to get the hell down off the wall. Then their custodial tools might be examined. Clunk! The canvas-wrapped tools went into the back of the van. They closed the doors, walked around the van in their khaki work outfits, and hopped in front. On the way to the gym, they talked about the Spanish Civil War as the radio played Bing Crosby.

11. At the gym

Ed had spent the afternoon running to get
extension cords for the movie projector,
and moving the projector and the screen
around. 5 O'clock was a bad time to show
a movie, with the light from the west windows slanting down and hitting the east
wall. Maybe Paulsen could just talk and
not show a movie, but, no, a filmed inter-
view with Groucho Marx was something
you didn't see every day. The west windows had no curtains and had never had
them. For indoor sports, that was good.
He moved the screen over to the west wall.
The podium and the basketball net board
in back of it were flooded with light, and
the east wall looked like another screen,
and here came people trooping in already.
They all sat down in the shady west wall
bleachers, and he knew they weren't going
to go sit on the east side where the sun
would blind them. He sighed, went to the
projector, and turned it. The basketball
net board was casting a shadow. He took
the screen and put it in the shadow. "Shit!
I'm screwed!" he muttered.

Five O'clock came. Sally Donaldson was
there in the shadows somewhere. Penny
McGee and her mom came in and scur-
ried to find a seat as the mayor stepped
into the sunlight and started things. He
spent some time talking about how he met
Jack Paulsen and how he had cracked up

when Paulsen's humor book came out in
'36. He'd read all of it, not just the jokes,
that were in a different type and easy to
find, and, darn it, it made sense! Jack...
say, wasn't there another Jack, named
Jack Benny? And Jack Paulsen was just
as funny. Sure he was! Jack Benny and
Jack Paulsen were both going to give Adolf
Hitler a gut punch, with comedy, which
he couldn't stand, if the U.S.A. ever had to
fight the Nazis. Yes, they would seriously
weaken him with American humor, before
American and English fighting men came
to deliver the knockout! And that would
be no joke! Heck, no!

Penny McGee felt a tap on her shoulder,
and looked around. There was Chester,
sitting there grinning, with his elbows on
his grasshopper knees. "We're the ones
that are going to clock Hitler!" he whis-
pered. "Mighty Joe Stalin, me, and Lu-
Ann! Ka-pow!"

Looking at the wall glare, then his watch,
the mayor delivered a long flowery introduction for his old buddy Paulsen.
Paulsen, when he got behind the microphone, looked both amused and affection-
ate. He started out by saying, "Let's have
a show of hands! How many of you have
read "Praise Of Folly" by Erasmus of Rot-
terdam?" Smiling glibly, he waved his own

hand in the air. No one else stirred. Sally Donaldson had read it, but she didn't want a bunch of men cow-eyeing her.

"Folks, when I tell you how humor works, and start pulling jokes apart, breaking them into their components, it's going to be about as funny as an autopsy class in medical school!" Everyone laughed, which put him off his rhythm. An autopsy class was funny? Well, OK, maybe it was!

"Uh...it'll be about as funny as a little boy torturing a bug!" The bleachers erupted in howls. Torturing a bug? Who were these people? They must really like torturing bugs! Yech!

"Why...it'll be about as funny as...what?... Marxism after I got through with it!" A roar came from the bleachers. Oh-ho-ho! Marxism in ruins! "Jeese!" said Paulsen. He was the only straight man in the room. The audience was tipping back, hooting at the ceiling, pounding their knees and their sides. He muttered, "Oh...my...dear...god! Am I in hell?"

"No, but you will be!" yelled a man's voice from the crowd. That was the final touch. People in the front row fell off the bench and rolled in the floor, howling.

Paulsen turned around. Shadows of 2

crouching gunmen froze, on the brightly
lit wall in back of him, as if hoping not
to be detected. The shadows cautiously
looked at each other, then turned their
heads toward Paulsen, and slowly hun-
kered down. A gale of laughter came from
the crowd as 2 other shadows appeared
at either side of the wall glare, and crept
toward the first 2 shadows, with pistols
extended. Sneak, sneak, sneak! Gonna
take 'm by surprise! The audience roared
again, some bellowing, some squeaking
harshly in the high registers. It was then
that Paulsen thought to look at the west
windows. The armed silhouettes were
ready to shoot, now. The prep guy silhouettes, standing next to them, noncha-
lantly tapped them on the shoulder. The
hit guys jerked, got real still, then looked
slowly up into the prep guys' gun barrels.
Their rifles cautiously went down, till they
could drop them, and their hands went up.
The crowd whistled and clapped, except
for Chester, who got up and stalked out.
"Don't leave mad!" called Jack Paulsen.

Ed the electrician walked over to the
mayor, who said, "Ed! You're radiant!
What's up, buddy!"

"Mayor, we can't fight the sun in Kansas in
August! What say we set this baby up in
your reception room and watch Groucho
there?"

Paulsen came up and slapped both men on the shoulder. "Sounds like a plan!" he said.

12. At the mayor's

"The big point I really would have made... the point...ah! Thanks!...Here's to Marxism!...The point, I say, is this: most jokes tell a story about some poor shmuck who thinks he's going to inherit the moon... that's why comedy is tragedy...anyway, he thinks he's going to win big, inherit a fortune, something nutty like that, and then his ridiculous hope gets shot down...bang! Set 'em up and shoot 'em down! Charlie was so good at that. Or

communism, say...now why's everyone laughing?"

Writer fussings

Paulsen is obviously based on Max Eastman. The background and character are fact-based, but all action and dialogue are fictional. I thought it would probably be unlikely that there would be a Kansas town named after a New England philosopher of the 1830's, so I went ahead with Brownson. Then a friend told me there really was a lefty town in Kansas in the 30s. Whaddaya know!

History of basketball in Kansas: up and going in '37. The events taking place from 2 p.m. to 5:30 p.m., Aug. 15, 1937 never happened. I was personally curious what might have happened to my characters after 1937.

Sally was glad she did it (had sex with Paulsen). She always thought it had freed her in some way, especially after reading Paulsen's book about the poetic mind.

Chester suffered a nervous breakdown after the Hitler-Stalin pact, left Lu-Ann and bummed around in California. In 1952 he voted for Eisenhower

Lu-Ann remained a Stalinist, though she did take down the John Reed Club sign after Chester left..

The mayor kept getting re-elected. His speeches got more and more corny.

The assistant mayor became a radio sports announcer, after serving as an army officer in the Pacific in WWII.

The two hit guys claimed to be misdirected hunters.

Penny continued what she was do-
ing. Lots more guys letched on her, but
learned their lesson when she decked
them. When her mom and Lu-Ann moved
into the room above the bookstore, she
and Henry started having kids.

The mom had to work in the bookstore
after Jerry joined the Navy. She knew
and cared zip about Communism.

Jack Paulsen got back some respect after
the Hitler-Stalin pact, and was solicited
for polit-articles by Look, Life, *and even*
Readers Digest. *He declined to join the*
New Center in '46. That would be joining,
wouldn't it? HUAC? Joe McCarthy and
the gang waved him through the check-
point, though he hated them. He didn't
have to spill, though there were plenty
of...whoa! Let's not get into that!

I thought I was through fussing, but one
of my characters wants to talk. She's
in her 90's now (in 2007), wears men's
clothes, and smokes a pipe. It's raining
outside the bookstore, which survived
HUAC, Reagan, tornadoes and the tea
party. Tea is in fact steaming in a clear
Russian tea glass sitting in a tarnished
silver holder on a book crate. "It wasn't
about Stalin," she says, "Hitler, Ribben-
trop, none of that, the gulags, nada. It

was about workers pushing back, making the plutocrats back down. Have you noticed that NPR is afraid to talk about Woody Guthrie now? Pathetic. You've given it all away, being reasonable. The '60's rad cream puffs talked about individuality. Well, let's see their great accomplishments. What I really miss is the big brotherhood, the callused hands picking you up and putting you back on your feet."

All right, this story is over. As you leave, please fold your chair and stack it over near the wall. Don't forget to visit the pamphlet table on the way out, and put a dollar in the jar.

Cocoon

"Hi! My name's Douglas!" A boy in a T-shirt and shorts stood behind the picket fence. "Want to see my yard and look at my toys?"

"OK." Mike went in at the gate. Douglas showed him around. There was a wagon, some swings, and a patch of sand where toy trucks had made roads. Mike squated down and rolled them along their roads and over rough spots that made them turn over.

Douglas said, "My dad is real important at the base! My mom is nice too. We have a TV! It's brand new. It's a Motorola. Wanna come in and see it?"

"Yeah!"

The two six-year-old boys climbed inside the trailer. Douglas' mom saw them and said, "Well howdy-do! Douglas has a new friend! What's your name, hon?"

"Mike." He tried to smile but it felt wrong. Douglas's mom wore a pretty dress and apron. The place was too clean.

"Mama, I'm going to turn on the TV." Mike flinched, expecting him to get slapped.

"You just go right ahead, sweety pie! I'll pour you both a glass of Kool Aid and make some nice sandwiches."

And that was it? She wasn't going to yell at him to keep his paws off the expensive TV?

Douglas put his dirty hand right on the TV knob and turned it. A greenish picture slowly phased in. The speakers buzzed. A man in a suit appeared on the screen, holding up a box of detergent and talking. Mike noticed the handkerchief sticking out of his front jacket pocket and wondered if it had snot on it. Douglas stood next to the TV smiling. "See? Now watch." He clicked the knob and the picture shrank into a bright greenish dot in the middle of the screen.

Douglas's mom, who was still smiling, as if she liked doing that, called from the kitchen, "Come have your Kool-Aid, Mikey! I made jelly and peanut butter sandwiches too!" She ruffled Douglas' hair as he ran and jumped into the wooden chair next to the beautiful polished table that had a lace doily in the middle with a vase of flowers.

Mike walked slowly toward the table like in a science fiction movie. Douglas's mom ruffled his hair too, and he jumped back, before she could hurt him. He tried to smile at her. That's what normal people did, wasn't it? The sandwich was of course delicious. He sure as hell didn't get sandwiches like that at home. But the crust of the white bread had been cut off. Some of the jelly got on his face because the crust wasn't there to stop it doing that. He saw Douglas's mom wiping Doug's face, and Doug liking it. He could be next, and she might not be so nice. So he quickly wiped the jelly off with his hand and wiped his hand on his pants while she wasn't looking.

After he and Douglas get through and ran out the door again, Mike said, "You know what sometimes hangs on fences? Cocoons! Let's look under the boards." He glanced out at the
desert just then, took a big breath of hot dusty air and smiled. He knew things Douglas didn't know. As Douglas excitedly followed him to look at the wiggly cringing things under the fence boards, he saw one of the toy trucks next to the patch of sand he was passing, and kicked it. The little men he imagined riding in it were all killed.

Cat

With the accident report sitting on the table between them the brothers talked about their sister Cat whose death was explained in the document.

Ralph said, "Remember when Cat was three years old, and used to like going on drives? She would sit on my lap and point out of the window. One time Mom stopped to look at some bluebonnets, and we all got out of the car to take pictures. I put Cattie in the flowers and Mom took a picture as she ran through them. She ran to me with her arms lifted to make me pick her up again. Then right away she squirmed and reached toward the car. She wanted to ride and point some more."

Terry reached across his donuts and turned the police report around so he could read it. "This piece of shit has nothing to do with Cat."

"No, this isn't like Cat."

"Remember when she was in kindergarten and the teacher gave all the little kids pictures of cartoon animals to color? They all got first prize certificates as little artists. Cataline brought home all the googly-eyed turkeys, dogs and rabbits, and I griped when the pictures got under my work boots cause she left them all over the

floor. I gathered them up and put them
in a cardboard box but later I could never
open that box without crying."

"When she was in fourth grade, she ran
and screamed and argued and acted
out till I yelled at her, and she cried and
sulked and drew back her fist to hit me."

"But after that she got religious. She went
and stood in a tank of water and was bap-
tised, with all the smiling church prople
around her. She went to teen events at
church and made lots of friends. The minister was proud of her. She raised money
for charity drives to help old people and
drug addicts."

"She would bring the church kids home
and they would sit around in the living
room and talk about the drug addicts they
tried to save. They would get to pretend-
ing they'd just come from a pot party, and
maybe had some heroin, some meth and
some crack."

"Remember when she quit religion, and
her minister came knocking at the door?
She shut him out just like she was shutting
us out. The minister stood on the porch
looking horrified. She wouldn't let anyone in her room, wouldn't say where she
had gone in the night and who she'd been
with."

"Ye'p! Then...she was gone, moved out, impossible to find for two years and finally there was the accident, and the funeral."

"What was the deal with that accident? It didn't make sense to me."

From talks with Cataline's former church friends the brothers knew some things. These friends had all been in the youth ministry and known Cataline there. One now worked as a stocker at Walmart. One was an ex-marine with part of an arm missing, and a sunken place in his head. One was a salesman at Suburban Honda. One was a sad-faced counter clerk at Salvation Army, a former addict. He's the one who knew and said the most. About himself. About the idea of telling the truth instead of lying. About how Cataline loved her brothers even though she ran from them. Ran from them because she loved them. About the nest.

The brothers with their long half-gray hair and their untucked Levi shirts stood in front of the glass counter at Salvation Army and talked to Larry the ex-addict. They listened while looking toward the front window that was bright with a view of passing cars on the main drag in Universal City. Larry would wind down and the brothers would look at his face and make him start talking again.

"The nest, Nate's nest out there..."

"Where?"

"Outside Cibolo."

"Nate. Who's that?"

"He used to be in the church, back when Cat was religious. You know, we did try to keep it up...Religion I mean. I made it back to Jesus recently. Nate went the other way, toward whatever. He wasn't alone. There was a bunch of losers out at that old abandoned house they took over. To be as sad as they were, they sure laughed a lot. Cataline went out there...

"To Nate.....

"...........

"Sorry, I was trying to picture it. She'd met Nate when we were volunteering at Windy Hollow Assisted Living Corp, back before the bad times, when we were still good. Out at Windy Hollow Nate volunteered in the kitchen and Cataline volunteered to talk with the residents. She reminded them, since they were forgetful, that Jesus loved them and she, Cataline, did too.

"The residents were happy to know this, but they especially wanted Cataline to bring her ear nice and close so they could tell her things that... maybe she hadn't realized. The love in her perky teenage eyes turned to surprise, fear and sadness. I could see Nate watching her from the kitchen door where he was propping his chin on a mop handle.

"When break time came, the assistant manager came out in a tie and a short sleeved white shirt and he made sure the church kids sat down and the cook fried 'em up some burgers. Cataline went right to Nate, who made her laugh. She needed a laugh about then. When she got back to the old people, she wasn't listening any-more.

"So you see...

"When Cataline showed up at Nate's nest three years later, she was accepted right into that bunch. She was Nate's special girl. No one better give her any shit. Not till Nate got through."

Larry saw the two dangerous-looking men on the other side of his counter get hard expressions. He said he'd never disre-spected Cataline. He was there at the nest hanging with the other low-lifes cause that's where they were all supposed to be. It was the one place in that whole god damn town where neighbors wouldn't call the police.

He said that seeing Cataline become tired and bitter, seeing her sell drugs, seeing her go into the upstairs room with one low-life or another to have sex, made him wonder if this was really what it all boiled down to.

The brothers were through with Larry. Walking out, Terry saw a shirt at the end of the rack, caught hold of it and turned it, looking for thin spots or grease marks. "Come on!" called Ralph from the door-way.

In the truck, Ralph said, "I was about to grab him and beat on him."

"Wasn't his fault."

"I know that."

They drove over to the Cibolo P.D. to get the printout of the the accident report. It said that Cat's body, fairly mashed up, dead as shit, had been taken directly to the morgue. The truck driver had been found sitting on the guard rail near where he'd hit her, with his face in his hands. The patrol car flasher lit him up.

Seven minutes before that, he'd parked his truck carefully, down the road a ways, before walking back and looking at what he'd done. He had an old style cell phone with an antenna, and he called the police on it. While describing where she was, he

noticed he hadn't yet put cones. She was
in the road. It was 3 a.m. but still someone might come along. He trotted back
to the truck, still talking to the police, got
the cones out, brought them back, and
put them, then sat down on the guard
rail. Metal was playing somewhere. He
looked over his shoulder and saw Nate's
nest, fairly close, with the windows lit. He
lowered his face into his hands again and...
ye'p!...that's when the police arrived.
As Terry read a technical description of
the various physical reasons why Cat was
dead, Ralph said, "Mama told me she paid
Cataline's co-pay. I asked her what that
was all about. She said Cat had had an
STD. I said, why in fuck didn't you tell
us then? She said we would have got in
trouble going out to that place."

"That's possible."

The brothers talked over Cataline's accident report.

"What was she doing walking in the road
at 3 in the morning?"

"On drugs, maybe. Didn't know where she
was. Didn't see the truck, or didn't care.
Truck didn't see her either. It was a blind
turn."

"Maybe she was escaping the gang. Maybe
they'd beat her up and she wasn't thinking

right."

"If they thought she was about to narc on em, they might have drugged her and <u>then</u> beat her

The brothers got up and walked out of the donut joint, into the blinding sun. They climbed into the truck. Terry asked, "When's the best time to go out to the nest?"

"Oh, maybe 10 tomorrow morning. Atom bomb wouldn't wake 'em then."

"I don't care if they're awake."

Back at the house, Mom was home, banging dishes in the kitchen. "Why?" she called out. "Why can't two grown men clean anything in this house?"

"Uh...sorry, Mom."

"Sorry."

Funny. They were both planning to commit murder, but they knew they really should have done those dishes.

At 10 o'clock the next morning, Ralph rolled himself out from under the '93 Taurus he was working on. He smiled, but his eyes flashed something unexpected for a moment. Terry had already washed

the grease off his hands, and stood wait-
ing. "Bill, we're going out for a while. Back
about 12."

Bill, the boss, said, "Get outa here, you
monkeys! Have a good time, whatever it
is."

In front of Nate's nest, they got out,
slammed the truck doors, didn't bother
being quiet. Stoners at 10:30. They took
the bundle out of the truckbed, took the
shop rags off, wiped down the guns, put on
cloth gardening gloves, the ones with green
dots, and took up the guns. They were
talking normally as they headed on in.

"Oo lordy!"

The couch was occupied by a sleeping bum
in his underwear with his cock hanging
out.

"He had some good dreams."

They walked up the stairs, its bannister
draped with dirty T-shirts and towels,
When they got upstairs they looked curi-
ously into doorways. They could smell a
backed-up toilet somewhere. In the first
room were two floor mattresses, boots,
smoking paraphernalia, rhinestone-cov-
ered woman jeans, panties, stench. Nate
and Barb were on a mattress, an easy shot
if there ever was one, but not yet. A tour

through the other bedrooms first. There they saw the rest of the gang of low-lifes, more or less dangerous when awake, but stupid looking while asleep.

"There's Linda over there."

"Yeah. Come on."

They turned around and went back down the stairs then out to the porch. They didn't have to hurry, with this trash. They plopped down in two porch chairs, and looked out at their truck which was ticking as its motor cooled.

"I could use a beer."

"The pause that refreshes."

"What really happened that night? A beating?"

"I've wondered that."

"If these fucks weren't dead, would they really be alive?"

"……"

"I mean like…what if we sentenced them to not be shot? Then they'd have to live with themselves a few more years."

"Something to think about."

They sat for a couple of minutes.

"Gonna be a hot one."

"Yeah."

Ralph thought of Cat again. "Love must be terrible."

"Huh? That's a funny thing to say."

"I know it's terrible. I'm not in doubt."

"Guess Cat thought so too."

After a while, they got up and left.

In the house, no one woke up for a long, long time.

Bullets And Horses

In the house the frontier family ate, the
sons with the newspaper near, their voices
like one plank rubbing against another.

From the barn, the horse had an opinion. (Here make a horse noise) (Heee-a-
houghhh! Something like that).

The daughter stared at her potatoes.

There were two of them. Which to eat
first?

The ghost helpfully pointed to one of the
potatoes. But was he right?

The ghost pretended to sit at the table, a
look of enterprise on his face, determined
to "eat."

After a while Paw stuck his knife in the
table. Doinnnggg!

The ghost stood up, turned around,
reached, took down his iron, looked at it,
sat down next to rags and oil, and cleaned
it.

Maw looked out the red window and saw
trouble boiling out of the distance. She
worried Paw and he glanced.
Ye'p! Raiders.

The ghost reached for bullets and "loaded"
the appliance. He snapped his iron closed
and spun the cylinder.

Paw turned his head and held his hand to
his eyes.

The raiders arrived. Their horses turned
around in the yard, their haunches appear-
ing in the window.

Paw got up, walked, opened the door.
Squinnnch!

He showed on the porch. His iron was
with him, perky in his hand.

The ghost got up and ambled out. He
sat down on the edge of the porch....just
kinda...slow and easy. Behind his shoulder, Maw's shotgun peeked out from the
shadow of the door.
In the yard, the raider boss, Jeth Varney
was continuing a yelled conversation with
the other outlaws.

He'd killed enough in his recent spree to
gain respect from the other wild psychopaths,

but lost it by asking too many questions
and by occasionally quoting Shakespeare.

Out on the trail, between crimes,
with the horse bouncing him up and down,

he'd yelled, "Hamlet was right! Or was he wrong?" He frowned and shook his head to get his thoughts right. That didn't work. He reached for his gun, extracted it and shot at something. Anything. A rock. Ping!

He asked Paw, "Settler, what can I do, now that I'm so turned around?"

Paw waved his hand disgustedly. There can't be questions in a story like this!

Varney turned to maw. She muttered and lowered her shotgun.

Varney turned to the ghost, who wasn't there. Varney fell off his horse.

Picture of Paw, glowering. Overvoice: "Paw later died from an overdose-a-corn-bread."

Picture of the sons, sitting at the table and holding newspapers. Overvoice: "The sons argued themselves to death. Their coffins were made of political planks. They couldn't be helped after that.

Picture of the daughter, looking slowly from one potato to the other. Overvoice: "After failing to understand the potatoes, the daughter turned to religion, but discovered there were many religions. She went to town and got stuck in the street between two churches. Nearby, Jeth Varney walked backwards into a saloon. Unfortunately, the daughter noticed this new angle to things. Was it a choice between two or a choice between three? And was the answer really to be found at the bottom of a whiskey bottle?"

Picture of the ranch house, Maw shakes her head. In the background the ghost shrugs and moves his mouth. Maw says, "I know what you mean."

Overvoice: Sometimes in the American West,

when the sun goes down,

a mystery remains.

There are ballads that will never have an ending. Others don't have a beginning, but have two endings. Others are without middles.

If you think about it, it's kinda messed up.

The Expatriate

Leaping onto the jet, the expatriate came to France, where the sneering American literary magazines would not extend the poisonous tentacles of their rejection notices (unless of course he sent them something).

At 2 the expatriate stepped out of his pension into the snooty French agora, carrying an envelope. The door woman raised an eyebrow.

After an annoyingly breezy walk through the village he came to the post office. Two old men on bikes stopped to stare. One muttered, "What the devil!" The other said, "It's the expatriate. That explains all!" The expatriate glared. "Objectificators!" he muttered, entering the post office.

A long line awaited him. "Maman! Look! The expatriate!" The mother applied hands to the child's eyes. Other patrons edged away from the expatriate, who glared at one and all.

Finally he reached the counter. "I wish, please, to purchase, how do you say, mailage, postage, whatever, and then to mail the envelope!"

Amazement showed on the postwoman's face. "What's that? You wish to mail your underwear?"

"No! Attawnsionne! The eeeeen-vel-ope!"

"I cannot be expected to understand such language!"

"The envelope! The envelope! The envelope!" While waving the envelope and jumping up and down, the expatriate noticed that he was nude. The cabal! The poison! "Sacred azure! They're here!" he said, assuming he was still speaking French. He used the envelope to cover his Etats Unis as he crab-walked toward the door, where a policeman waited to assist him.   "Oh, you Indiana Reviews! You Atlantics! You haven't published geniuses like me in 20 years! Did you like your trip to France? Rejecting me must be the most delightful of drugs, you...you Paris Reviews!"

At his pension where he surprised the door woman with his attire, a blanket loaned by the police, he discovered that mail had arrived. Marked with the names of prestigious U.S. literary journals, it was not really mail. It was snakes, spiders, madness.

The expatriate's next destination would be Japan. He had secretly begun practicing tea ceremonies. Perhaps while he hid in

Osaka, a missile would arrive from North Korea. He would welcome it, so long as it did not pop open above the city, spilling letters from prestigious U.S. literary journals rejoicing at the opportunity of having read his moving and excellent poem, but explaining that it was not a good fit for issue 37, 38 or 39.

A moment later the door woman was astonished to see a human jackrabbit with a suitcase exiting the front door and heading for the airport. She noted with relief that he was wearing clothes.

Artists in the Underworld
by
Richard Wayne Horton

Richard's first book published with Human Error Publishing.

Praise For Richard Wayne Horton's Writing

"...With dream magic, cinematographic closeups an dissolves, Horton takes readers on a romp..." - Elizabeth MacDuffie, editor of Meat For Tea The Valley Review, and Meat For Tea Press.

"Like the way any self-respecting listener of jazz can recognize a Miles Davis solo within the first three notes, one can recognize a Richard Wayne Horton story within the first three sentences..." –Joshua Michael Stewart, author of Break Every String (poetry).

"...blends the other worldly and the ordinary, exposing the fantastical in the smallest moments of interpersonal connections..."
                    –Jacqueline Sheehan, NY Times bestselling author.

"...razor-sharp language that is both spare and beautiful..."
                    –Amy Laprade, author of So Nice To Finally Meet You (novel).

"Richard has found an amazing form for his work...loaded with texture and temperature and personality and sound...this is about an ideosyncratic America...or say, a Midwestern gothic." –Beth Filson, writer and artist.

"Horton's writing is escapist, but in a different way...While it may not have been the author's intention, these stories pare well with a perfectly prepared gin martini. There is this other world which Horton creates that seems to replicate ordinary reality, but is definitely another place."
                    –George J. Woodruff, writer.

"...a modern Poe?...Richard says a story 'is a root system'...the trunk and limbs that arrive from his roots bear fruit that is bittersweet. You're afraid to keep climbing and eating it, but you can't help yourself."
                    –John Burroughs, author of Rattle & Numb (poetry)